DRAGONS AROUND THE WORLD

For Otto and Sienna. A legacy of the 'dragon game'. — SAN

To my nephew Tommaso, who showed me that dragons are real if you know how to look for them. — MFM

First published in the United Kingdom in 2026 by Thames & Hudson Ltd, 6–24 Britannia Street, London WC1X 9JD

Consultancy by Heinz Insu Fenkl, Alexandra Green, Bella Myŏng-wŏl Dalton-Fenkl, Zara Fleming, Nicole-Rachelle Moore, Joe Nickols, Tania Roxborogh, Antony Wynn

EU Authorized Representative: Interart S.A.R.L.
19 rue Charles Auray, 93500 Pantin, Paris, France
productsafety@thameshudson.co.uk
interart.fr

A CIP catalogue record for this book is available from the British Library

ISBN 978-0-500-65401-9
01

Printed and bound in China by Toppan Leefung Limited

MIX
Paper | Supporting responsible forestry
FSC® C104723

DRAGONS AROUND THE WORLD

Sally A. Nicholls
Maria Francesca Melis

t&h

CONTENTS

INTRODUCTION 7

LINDWORM 8
The Venomous Dragon, Germany and Scandinavia

RYUJIN 10
The King of the Sea, Japan

QUETZALCOATL 12
The Feathered Serpent, Mexico

HYDRA 14
The Many-Headed Beast, Greece

LONG 16
The Imperial Dragon, China

DRAC 18
Fire-Breathing Monster, Spain

AIDO-HWEDO 20
Serpent Coiled Around the Earth, Benin

Y DDRAIG GOCH 22
The Red Dragon, Wales

LEVIATHAN 24
The Whale-Eater, Mediterranean Sea

DRACO 26
The Elephant Hunter, Ethiopia and India

DRUK 28
Generator of Storms, Bhutan

TANIWHA 30
Water Guardians, Aotearoa New Zealand

AZHDAHA 32
Mean, Fighting Machine, Iran

YONG 34
The Kind Dragon, Korea

NAGA 36
Royal Dragon, Southeast Asia

DRAGON MUSEUM 38
How we know what we know about dragons

Glossary 46

Index 47

About the Author and Illustrator 48

INTRODUCTION

A dragon is a reptile of awesome power. The word comes from the Latin for 'huge serpent'. Dragons can be found in stories and legends from across the globe. Their history is our history. From palaces in the clouds to deep ocean caves, dragons inhabit every part of the world. Their power must be respected, because although dragons can be dangerous, they are not necessarily evil. Many are benevolent and protective.

There are dragons that breathe fire and cause destruction, dragons that create life and bring good luck, dragons that guard treasure and dragons that control the tides and the weather. In this book we will bring these dragons to life.

You will learn how to recognise many kinds of dragons, from the colour of their scales to the number of claws they have. Discover where in the world they live, from Northern Europe to the forests of Ethiopia and from the heights of the Himalayas to the jungles of Mexico. Marvel at their abilities and understand why humans have admired and worshipped them for centuries.

LINDWORM

THE VENOMOUS DRAGON

WHO? Hoarder of treasure
WHAT? Malevolent forest serpent
WHERE? Germany and Scandinavia

ROLLING DANGER

The lindworm is a giant forest serpent with no legs, only two arms with long, sharp claws and small wings. They live between or under piles of rocks in the forest. Lindworms slither like snakes, using their arms to help pull themselves along. Some grow very, very long and when hunting, swallow their own tails to form a wheel and roll very fast at their prey. Lindworms are often found guarding mounds of treasure, which they use as their beds. But beware! The treasure is cursed and will bring no good to anyone who steals it.

DRAGON POWER!

Whatever lies beneath a lindworm grows as the dragon grows. That is why they collect treasure – as it increases under them, they become richer.

NOT QUITE INVINCIBLE

When facing a lindworm, it is important to use a shield. They spit a milk-like poison that can blind a person. It is very difficult to kill a lindworm. There is only one place on its body not protected by impenetrable scales: a small, soft spot of skin on its belly. It is only by stabbing this exact spot with a sword that a lindworm can be killed.

MAGICAL BLOOD

One of the most famous lindworms was Fafnir, who had a great hoard of gold. He was killed by the hero Sigurd, who lay in a pit and stabbed the lindworm's soft spot from underneath. Sigurd then dipped his fingers in the dragon's blood and tasted it. Miraculously, he found he could understand the language of the birds – a gift that saved his life when he heard the birds say that his accomplice Regin planned to kill him and steal Fafnir's gold.

RYUJIN

THE KING OF THE SEA

WHO? Underwater royal ruler
WHAT? Sea serpent with a pearl in each claw
WHERE? Japan

PEARLY CONTROL FREAK

In historic Japan, Ryujin is best known as the King of the Sea. He lives in a palace under the ocean, built from red and white coral. Other sea creatures such as turtles, fish and jellyfish act as his messengers and servants. Ryujin has strong legs for swimming, a long snake-like body, a wispy beard and whiskers. In each of his front claws he holds a pearl – one white and one blue. These pearls control the tides. The white pearl causes the tide to retreat, and the blue pearl makes it come in.

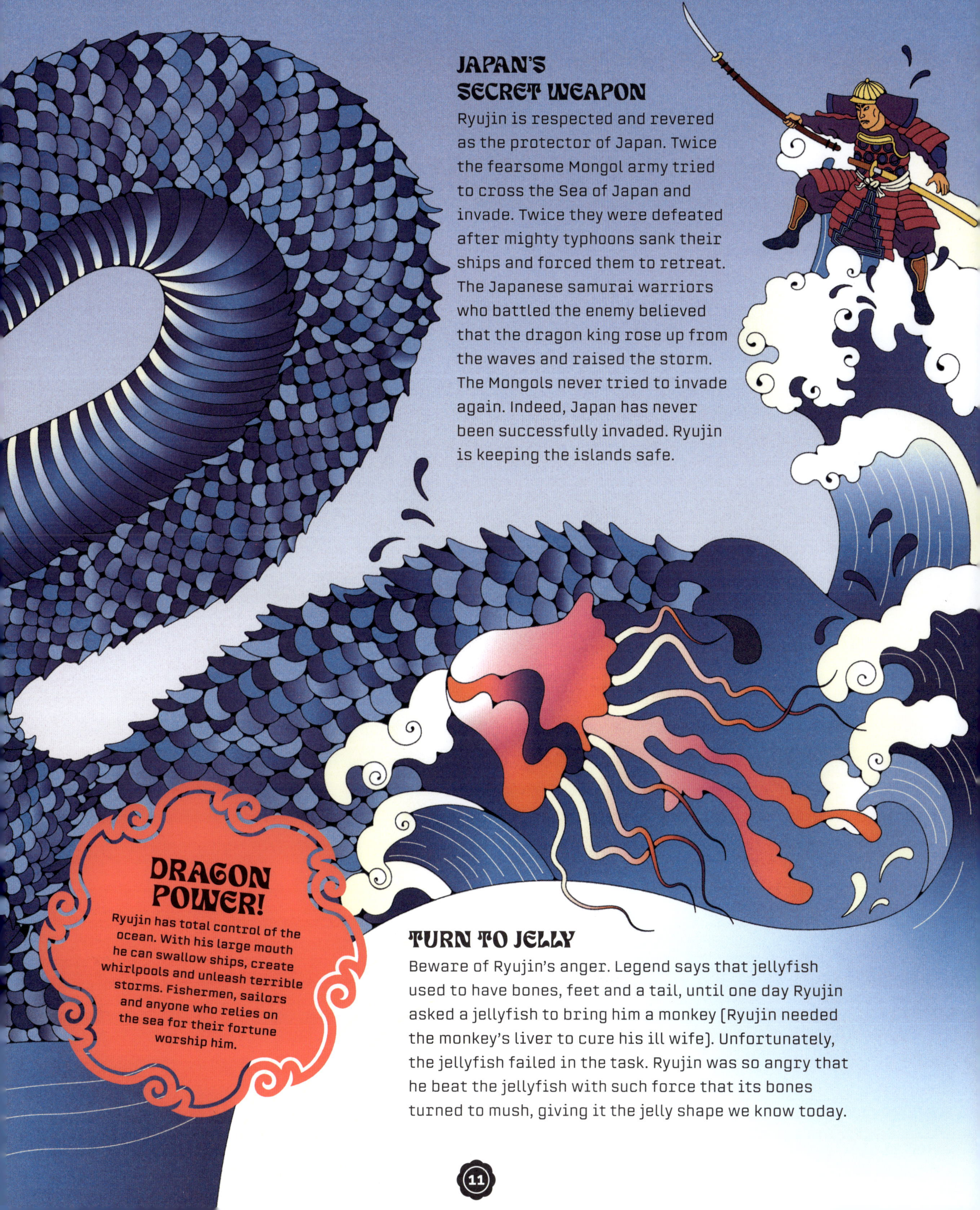

JAPAN'S SECRET WEAPON

Ryujin is respected and revered as the protector of Japan. Twice the fearsome Mongol army tried to cross the Sea of Japan and invade. Twice they were defeated after mighty typhoons sank their ships and forced them to retreat. The Japanese samurai warriors who battled the enemy believed that the dragon king rose up from the waves and raised the storm. The Mongols never tried to invade again. Indeed, Japan has never been successfully invaded. Ryujin is keeping the islands safe.

DRAGON POWER!

Ryujin has total control of the ocean. With his large mouth he can swallow ships, create whirlpools and unleash terrible storms. Fishermen, sailors and anyone who relies on the sea for their fortune worship him.

TURN TO JELLY

Beware of Ryujin's anger. Legend says that jellyfish used to have bones, feet and a tail, until one day Ryujin asked a jellyfish to bring him a monkey (Ryujin needed the monkey's liver to cure his ill wife). Unfortunately, the jellyfish failed in the task. Ryujin was so angry that he beat the jellyfish with such force that its bones turned to mush, giving it the jelly shape we know today.

QUETZALCOATL

THE FEATHERED SERPENT

WHO? Creator of the universe, that's who!
WHAT? Half-bird, half-snake and 100% dragon
WHERE? Mexico

IS IT A BIRD? OR IS IT A SNAKE? NO! IT'S A DRAGON!

Quetzalcoatl means 'feathered serpent' in Nahuatl, an indigenous language of Mexico and Central America. 'Quetzal' is a bird and 'coatl' means snake. Indeed, Quetzalcoatl has the body of a huge rattlesnake, but instead of being covered with scales, he has bright blue-green feathers. The feathers are like those found on the resplendent quetzal bird. He also has a long beak-like mouth with sharp, pointed teeth – there's no mistaking that he's completely dragon.

DRAGON POWER!

Wind is one of Quetzalcoatl's strongest powers. He uses the wind and his beak to sweep the land clean before the rain gods get to work washing it. Some say that when the sky grows dark, Quetzalcoatl's thunder rumbles and when the wind roars, it is because he is angry.

CREATOR AND CHILD-EATER

As if he isn't busy enough as the creator of the universe, Quetzalcoatl is also the god of knowledge, the inventor of books and the calendar, and the protector of priests. As an example of his protective instincts, he gave mankind the gift of maize, or corn – their main source of food. In return, the Aztecs offered up human sacrifices to please Quetzalcoatl and gain more favours. In essence, he ate his own children.

THE BONE COLLECTOR

Quetzalcoatl was worshipped by the Aztecs and before them, by the rulers of the mighty city of Teotihuacan in Mexico, where a six-tiered pyramid was built in his honour. There is no limit to the dragon's strength and intelligence. As a creator of the universe, he is responsible for both life and death. The Aztec creation myth describes how Quetzalcoatl descended to the underworld, known as Mictlan, to collect the bones of dead creatures. He then mixed his own blood with these bones to create the first humans. Mmmm, yum!

HYDRA

THE MANY-HEADED BEAST

WHO? Monster of the swamps
WHAT? Multi-headed water snake
WHERE? Greece

TOXIC FAMILY

According to Greek myth, Hydra lived in the marshes of Lerna in Greece near the entrance to the underworld. She was the child of the multi-headed giant serpent Typhon and Echidna, a monster who was half-woman and half-snake. She had a giant snake-like body ['hydra' means 'water snake' in ancient Greek] and nine heads – something she inherited from her father. From her mother, Hydra inherited her poison. Hydra's blood was so poisonous that even the smell of it could be fatal. She could also spit deadly acid.

DRAGON POWER!

Hydra couldn't be killed by just cutting off one of her heads. Each time a head was cut off, two more would grow in its place.

HEROIC HERCULES

When the great Greek hero Hercules committed a crime, he was given seven labours, or tasks, as punishment. The second of these was to kill Hydra. Hercules covered his mouth and nose to protect himself from her poisonous fumes. But for every head he cut off, two more grew back. Luckily for Hercules, his nephew Iolaus came to his aid. Each time Hercules cut off a head, Iolaus burnt the stump with a flame to stop another head from growing. Eventually they defeated her.

BLOODY AFTERLIFE

Once Hydra was dead, Hercules collected her poisonous blood to dip his arrows in. He used these toxic arrows to kill other monsters, including the dragon Ladon. Hydra lives on in another way, too. The goddess Hera, who disliked Hercules for killing Hydra, was so upset that she took Hydra's body and placed her in the sky as a constellation. Look up on a clear night, perhaps you'll be able to see a snake-like pattern of stars!

LONG

THE IMPERIAL DRAGON

WHO? Bringer of good fortune
WHAT? Dancer of air and water
WHERE? China

DRAGON POWER!

Long dragons carry a pearl under their throat that symbolises wealth, wisdom and knowledge. If a human ever gets to temporarily own a long's pearl, it will bring them great riches.

BRINGERS OF PROSPERITY

In Chinese legend, long dragons are wise and powerful guardians of the rivers and seas. During the winter they live underwater on the floors of lakes or oceans. Then in the spring, they leap up to fly and dance in the sky, forming clouds to water the land. Long are kind and helpful, but they can also be lazy. Disasters like floods, tidal waves and droughts can happen when they fall asleep and forget to keep an eye on things!

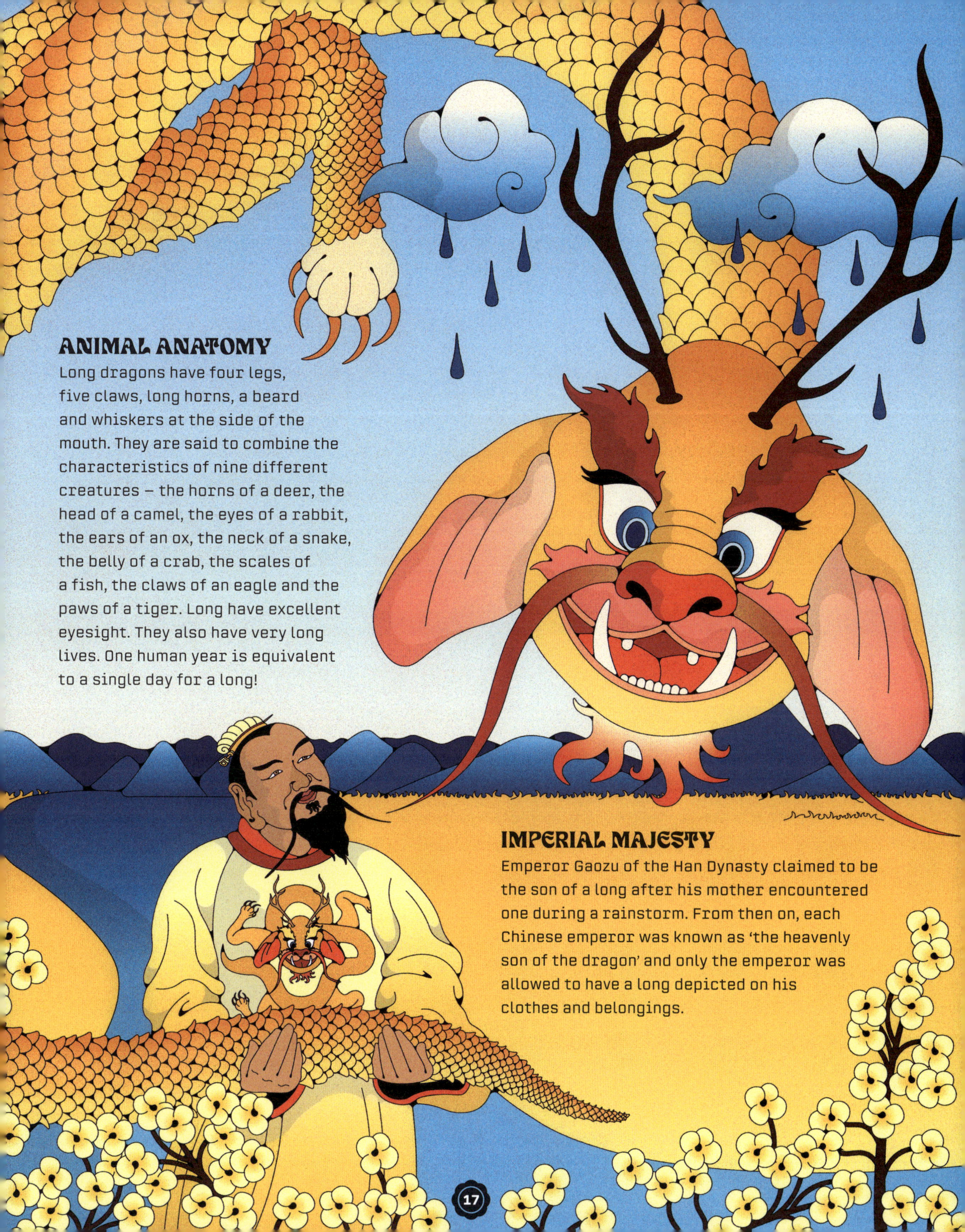

ANIMAL ANATOMY

Long dragons have four legs, five claws, long horns, a beard and whiskers at the side of the mouth. They are said to combine the characteristics of nine different creatures – the horns of a deer, the head of a camel, the eyes of a rabbit, the ears of an ox, the neck of a snake, the belly of a crab, the scales of a fish, the claws of an eagle and the paws of a tiger. Long have excellent eyesight. They also have very long lives. One human year is equivalent to a single day for a long!

IMPERIAL MAJESTY

Emperor Gaozu of the Han Dynasty claimed to be the son of a long after his mother encountered one during a rainstorm. From then on, each Chinese emperor was known as 'the heavenly son of the dragon' and only the emperor was allowed to have a long depicted on his clothes and belongings.

DRAC

FIRE-BREATHING MONSTER

WHO? Terror of the countryside
WHAT? Mighty killing machine
WHERE? Spain

A TASTE FOR FLESH

Drac had strong wings, mighty claws, many teeth, could breathe fire and had a taste for human flesh. Drac chose to make his home in the Catalan countryside near Barcelona. The local inhabitants were understandably terrified of him. To appease Drac and stop him from killing everyone in the area, they selected a different person each day to sacrifice to the beast – one person a day was better than twenty a day! The choice was made by lot – each person drew a straw and whoever had the shortest straw was the victim.

DRAGON POWER!

Unsurprisingly given his diet, he stank of rotting meat. This stink was so powerful it could rot anything near it. Protective armour was therefore a must when confronting him!

HIS COME-UPPANCE

One day it was the turn of the daughter of the local king to be sacrificed to Drac, but, luckily for her, that was the day the brave and handsome knight St Jordi rode into town. He saved her, and the rest of the population, by riding out in full armour to fight Drac. He triumphed by driving his spear through the dragon's throat.

A GIFT OF DRAGON BLOOD

As Drac lay dying, his blood seeped into the earth and on that spot a beautiful rose bush grew. Every year in April it bloomed with blood-red roses. In Catalonia they celebrate St Jordi and his defeat of Drac on the 23rd April, and it is traditional to give a rose to the people you love. Would you like a rose grown from a dragon's blood?

AIDO-HWEDO

SERPENT COILED AROUND THE EARTH

WHO? Maker of mountains
WHAT? Iron-eating giant
WHERE? Benin, West Africa

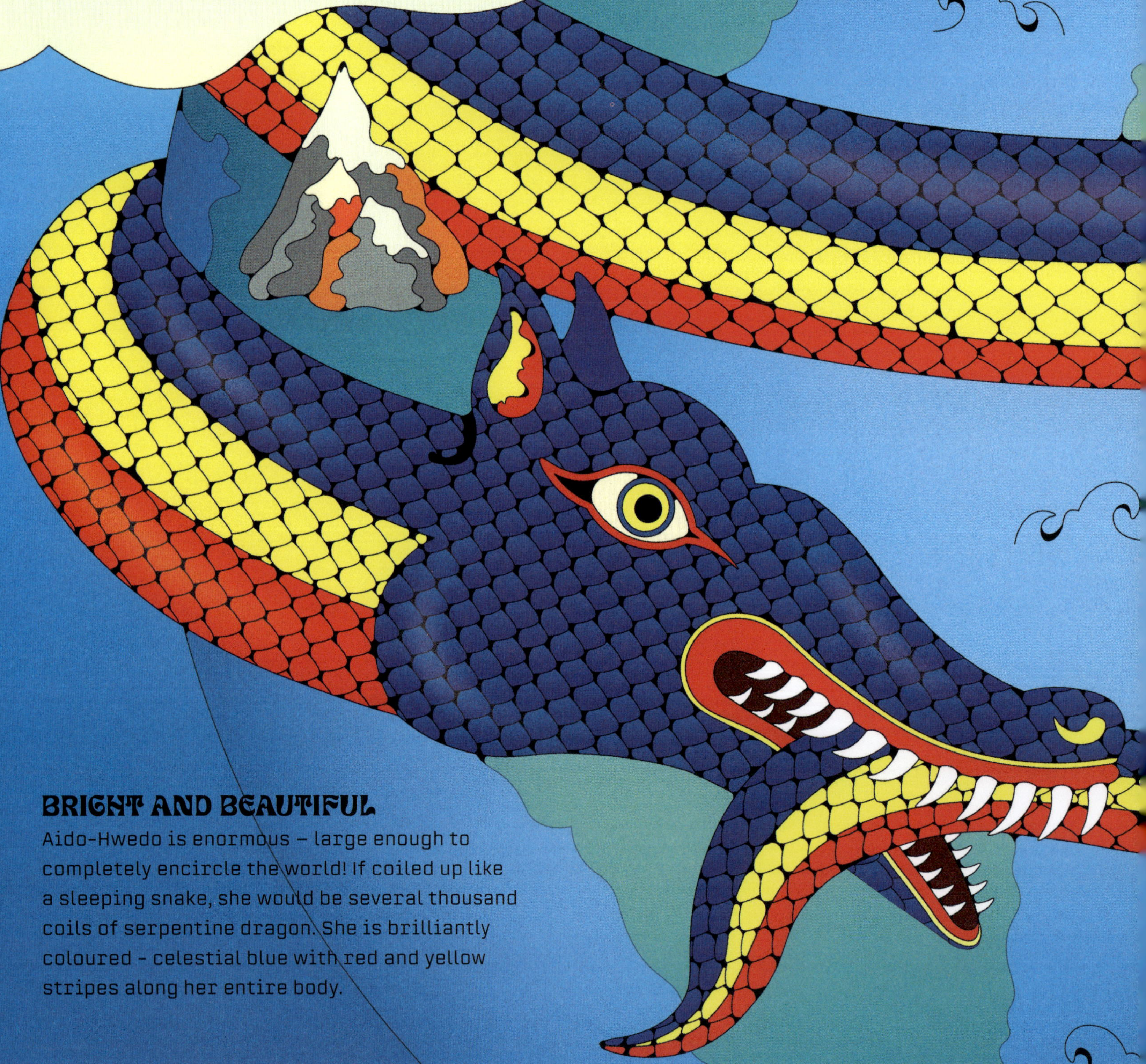

BRIGHT AND BEAUTIFUL

Aido-Hwedo is enormous – large enough to completely encircle the world! If coiled up like a sleeping snake, she would be several thousand coils of serpentine dragon. She is brilliantly coloured – celestial blue with red and yellow stripes along her entire body.

BEARING THE WEIGHT OF THE WORLD

At the beginning of time, the creator deity Mawu-Lisa was carried by Aido-Hwedo as they made the universe together. The winding movement of Aido-Hwedo's body formed the valleys, riverbeds and shapes of the earth. When the world was finished, it contained so many things – surely it would topple over?! Mawu-Lisa asked Aido-Hwedo to coil around the bottom of the earth to hold it steady. So that the world doesn't slip, Aido-Hwedo holds the tip of her tail in her mouth. Occasionally she gets uncomfortable and has to move, triggering earthquakes.

HUNGER FOR IRON

Aido-Hwedo's preferred meal is iron – lots and lots of iron. She needs it to keep up her strength. She feeds on an enormous supply of iron found in the earth. If that runs out, she will be forced to eat her own tail and then the world will collapse into the oceans.

DRAGON POWER!

A giant dragon means giant poo! Each night before Aido-Hwedo and Mawu-Lisa rested from their work creating the world, Aido-Hwedo would produce huge piles of poo. Eventually these became mountains containing the world's precious minerals like diamonds and gold.

Y DDRAIG GOCH

THE RED DRAGON

WHO? Welsh guardian
WHAT? Small but feisty, crimson warrior
WHERE? Wales, UK

DRAGON POWER!

Y Ddraig Goch is an indefatigable fighter, meaning that he never gives up. He was smaller than the white dragon but fought longer and harder until he won.

BATTLING HISTORY

Many, many centuries ago, the Celtic king Vortigern was trying to build a castle on Dinas Emrys – a hill in Snowdonia, Wales. But every day the castle collapsed. The king sought the advice of his magician, Merlin, who told him he would find the answer by digging underneath the hill. Sure enough, deep below the hill in an underground lake, Vortigern discovered a red dragon and a white dragon fiercely fighting one another, causing the castle's foundations to shake. The dragons were released into the open and continued to fight. Y Ddraig Goch eventually won and Vortigern was finally able to build his castle.

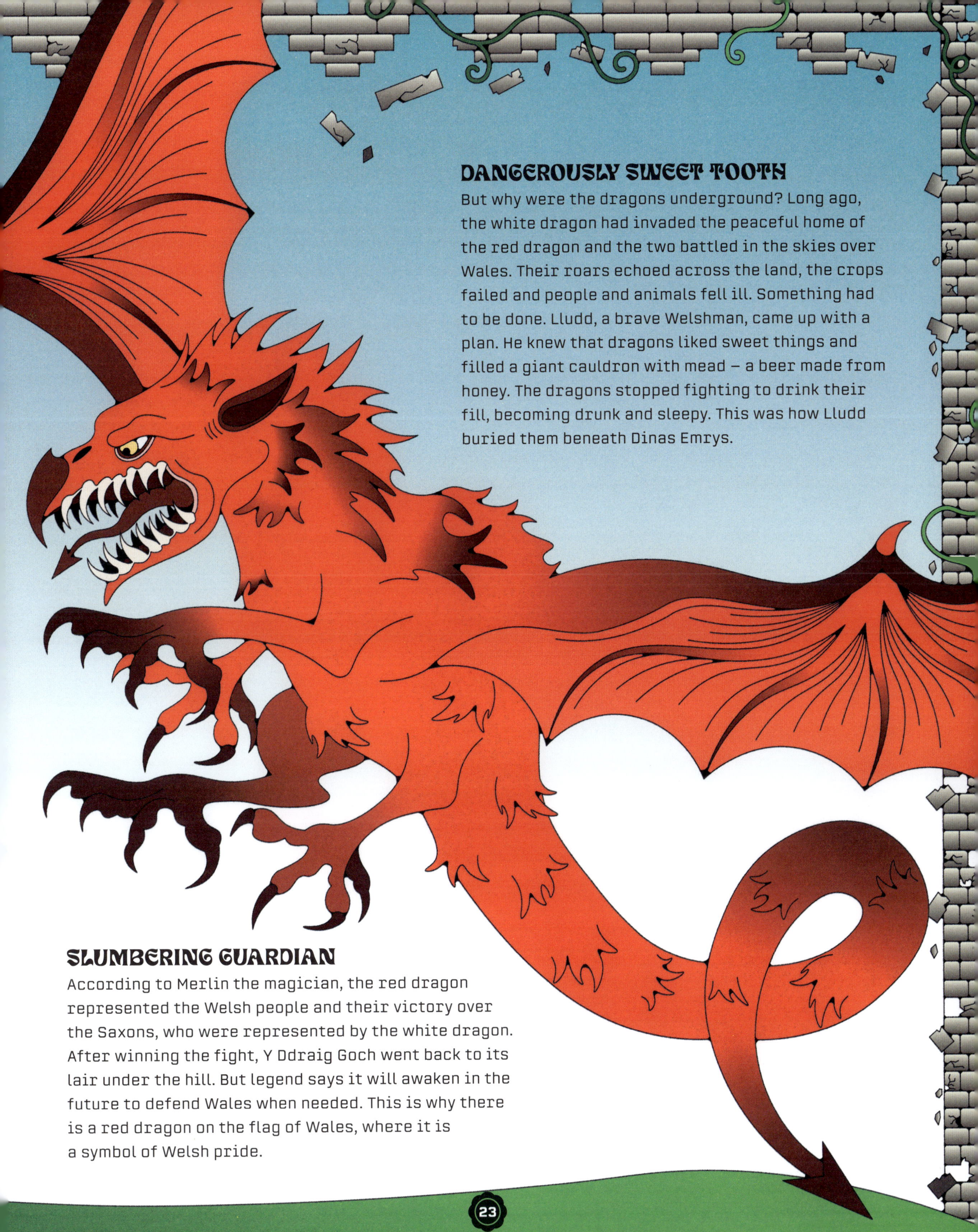

DANGEROUSLY SWEET TOOTH

But why were the dragons underground? Long ago, the white dragon had invaded the peaceful home of the red dragon and the two battled in the skies over Wales. Their roars echoed across the land, the crops failed and people and animals fell ill. Something had to be done. Lludd, a brave Welshman, came up with a plan. He knew that dragons liked sweet things and filled a giant cauldron with mead – a beer made from honey. The dragons stopped fighting to drink their fill, becoming drunk and sleepy. This was how Lludd buried them beneath Dinas Emrys.

SLUMBERING GUARDIAN

According to Merlin the magician, the red dragon represented the Welsh people and their victory over the Saxons, who were represented by the white dragon. After winning the fight, Y Ddraig Goch went back to its lair under the hill. But legend says it will awaken in the future to defend Wales when needed. This is why there is a red dragon on the flag of Wales, where it is a symbol of Welsh pride.

LEVIATHAN

THE WHALE-EATER

WHO? Demon of chaos
WHAT? Monstrous dragon of the sea
WHERE? Mediterranean Sea

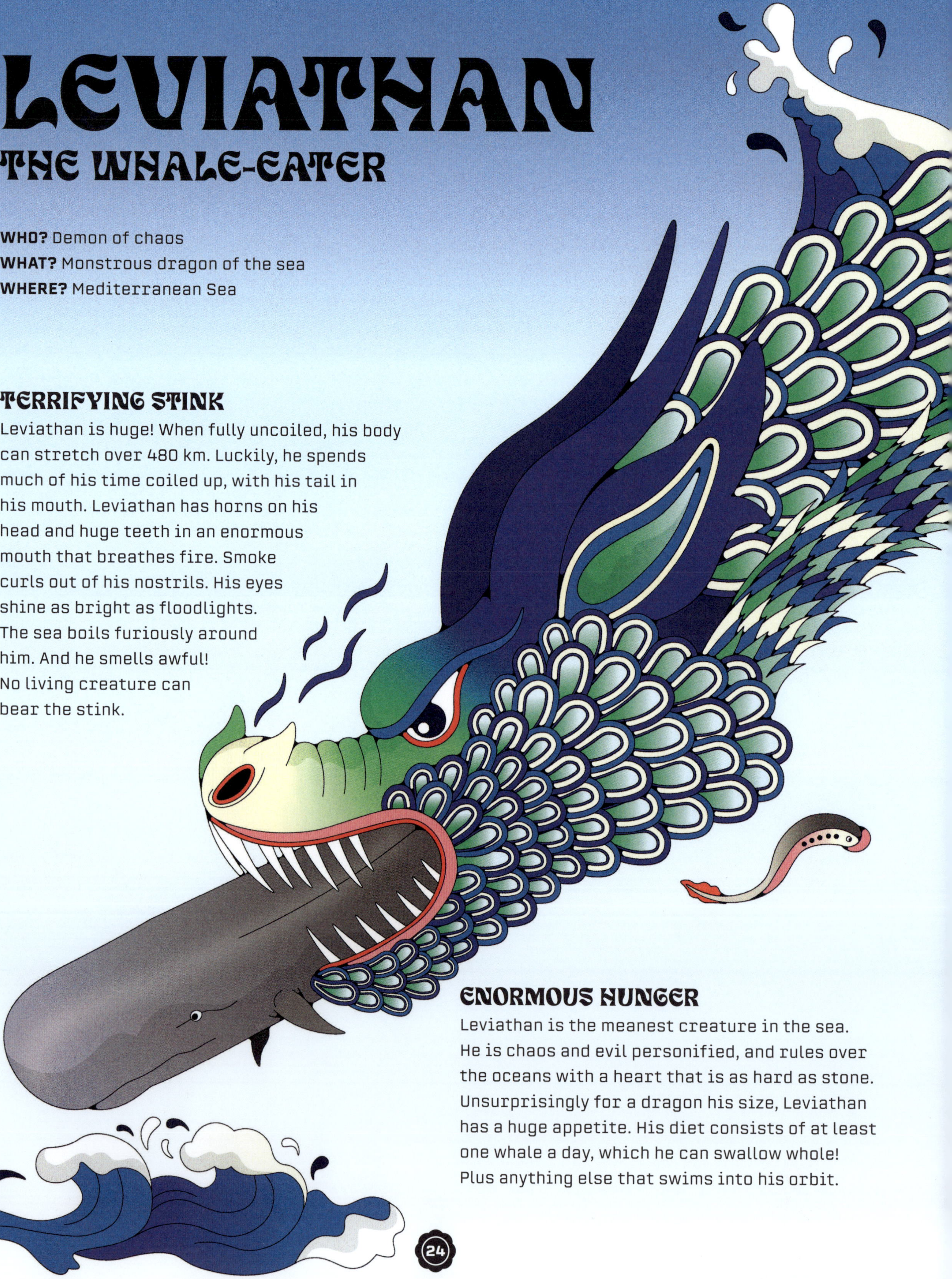

TERRIFYING STINK

Leviathan is huge! When fully uncoiled, his body can stretch over 480 km. Luckily, he spends much of his time coiled up, with his tail in his mouth. Leviathan has horns on his head and huge teeth in an enormous mouth that breathes fire. Smoke curls out of his nostrils. His eyes shine as bright as floodlights. The sea boils furiously around him. And he smells awful! No living creature can bear the stink.

ENORMOUS HUNGER

Leviathan is the meanest creature in the sea. He is chaos and evil personified, and rules over the oceans with a heart that is as hard as stone. Unsurprisingly for a dragon his size, Leviathan has a huge appetite. His diet consists of at least one whale a day, which he can swallow whole! Plus anything else that swims into his orbit.

DRAGON POWER!

Leviathan has impenetrable scales as large as shields that overlap across his back. His belly scales are as hard and sharp as broken pots. Arrows, swords and harpoons bounce off his body.

UNLIKELY PHOBIA

Despite his power, size and armoured body, Leviathan is not fearless. His one fear is a small worm called a 'kilbit', which clings to the gills of large fish and kills them. The Old Testament in the Bible states that only Yahweh [God] can defeat Leviathan. It is written that when he does so, Leviathan's skin will adorn the walls of Jerusalem and his flesh will be served in heaven as a sumptuous banquet.

DRACO

THE ELEPHANT HUNTER

WHO? The largest land dragon of all
WHAT? Flying python with poisonous pee
WHERE? Ethiopia and India

DRAGON POWER!

A draco's strength is in its rear end. It fights its enemies by thrashing them with its tail, and – like a python – kills by squeezing prey in its coils.

A BIT BATTY

Living within caves in Ethiopia and India is where one finds the draco dragon – the largest species of dragon found on land. This fearsome creature is huge. It can grow up to 55 m long – nearly twice the size of a blue whale. The draco has excellent eyesight, wings like a bat, a crest on its head, a small mouth, narrow nostrils and stiff pointed ears or horns. Oh, and a crushing tail.

ELEPHANT HATER

Elephants and dracos hate each other. According to medieval bestiaries, dracos are the only creatures capable of killing an elephant. First, the draco lurks in trees and then leaps out at the passing elephant, wrapping its tail around it and squeezing it to death. But this isn't always the best strategy. There is a risk that if the elephant falls over as it dies, and the draco hasn't kept its head and upper body out of the way, the elephant could land on the dragon, killing it at the same time.

POISONOUS PEE

Like many dragons, a draco breathes fire, but it does not have a poisonous bite. The same cannot be said for its urine! If a person were unlucky enough to walk beneath a flying draco as it peed, their skin would putrefy and peel off. In medieval times, the only way to protect against this was by rubbing one's skin with a paste made from prickly nettles soaked in vinegar. Smelly and uncomfortable.

DRUK

GENERATOR OF STORMS

WHO? Destroyer of lies and deliverer of truth
WHAT? Flying storm lizard with a mighty roar
WHERE? Bhutan

DRAGON POWER!

The thunder of Druk's roar is not just a sign of a storm. It is also a wake-up call that helps people break free from delusions and lies to see the truth.

TEMPESTUOUS MOUNTAINEER

Druk lives high up in the Himalayas, the tallest mountains in the world. He is a creature of the loftiest peaks and doesn't like to visit the lower slopes. Many Himalayan people claim to have seen him taking off from the highest pastures and soaring into the atmosphere. Druk is the creator of storms. As he lifts off from the ground and rises into the sky, the wind gets stronger, the clouds quickly gather and violent storms roll across the peaks. When he roars, thunder echoes through the mountains.

DESIRABLE JEWELS

He is slightly smaller than the Chinese long, though otherwise a similar shape. He is brightly coloured, often orange or red. In each of his claws he clutches a jewel. These represent long life, wealth, wisdom and strength. Druk is a bringer of good fortune. A gentle and generous dragon despite his mighty roar.

LAND OF THE THUNDER DRAGON

According to legend, a long time ago a Buddhist monk was visiting Southern Tibet, China, following instructions to set up a monastery there. When he arrived, he saw nine dragons taking off into the sky, creating a loud clap of thunder. He then named his practice of Buddhism after the Druk dragon. This form of Buddhism later spread to Bhutan, where the Bhutanese called their country 'Druk Yul' which means 'Land of Druk' in Dzongkha, the official language of Bhutan. Druk protects the land and people from harm, which is why he appears on the country's flag.

TANIWHA

WATER GUARDIANS

WHO? Dragon of the South Pacific
WHAT? Shape-changing water reptile
WHERE? Aotearoa New Zealand

EARTH-MOVING GIANTS

Gigantic reptiles with fiery eyes, lashing tails and sharp teeth, taniwha are powerful guardians not to be messed with! They protect the land and work to keep a balance between people and nature. Their lairs are in deep pools and underwater caves. Taniwha have immense strength: Wellington (the capital of Aotearoa New Zealand) Harbour was once a lake until two taniwhas, Ngake and Whātaitai, broke through the cliffs and opened an entrance from the lake to the sea.

TRIBAL GUARDIANS

Some Māori tribes believe that the taniwha swam alongside the canoes of their Polynesian ancestors as they travelled to Aotearoa New Zealand. Each taniwha was the guardian of a particular canoe. Once the people had settled in the new land, the taniwha continued to protect the families that were in their canoe. So long as the taniwha are respected, the members of that tribe can live in harmony with the taniwha, the land and each other. If anyone upsets the balance and the taniwha believe a place is disrespected or a boundary crossed, they may react with force to resolve it.

DRAGON POWER!

Taniwha are shape-changers. In the deep oceans they can take the form of sharks or whales. They can even disguise themselves as harmless floating logs.

TRAPPING A TANIWHA

There was once a taniwha called Te Tau-a-Porirua who killed many people. A chief named Tara set a trap for it. He wanted to restore safety to the land. He made a giant eel pot, put 200 dogs inside as bait and then set the pot in the lake. The taniwha thought the dogs would make a good snack and entered the trap. Tara dragged the pot to shore and killed Te Tau-a-Porirua. He cut open the stomach of the taniwha, and the bodies of more than 200 people were found inside!

AZHDAHA

MEAN, FIGHTING MACHINE

WHO? Creator of chaos
WHAT? Fire-breathing lizard
WHERE? Iran

EVOLVING INTO A DRAGON

The azhdaha is a huge lizard with a long scaly body, four legs like a lion, small wings and a head like a wolf with a long snout. It has blazing eyes and a wide mouth that can breathe fire. Most azhdaha start their life as snakes, but if they live over a hundred years and grow really big, they can mutate into dragons.

DRAGON POWER!

Not only can they breathe fire, but when an azhdaha gets angry, flames flicker along the length of their body. This makes them difficult to fight!

NOT TO BE MESSED WITH

The azhdaha is mean and wily. They lust for power and are a threat to humanity. Azhdaha can spit poison and swallow their prey (men and horses) whole. They bring chaos and confusion to the world. Persians rode into battle with banners depicting the dragons to terrify their enemies. The hero Rostam had such a banner and it was so large it seemed to eclipse the sun.

DEFEATED BY TEAMWORK

One night as the hero Rostam slept, a monstrous dragon called Asdeev crept towards him. Luckily Rostam's faithful horse Rakhsh saw Asdeev and woke his master. But the night was dark and the dragon disappeared into the gloom. This happened twice more. On the third occasion, Rakhsh tried to chase the monster away. The dragon roared and flames came out of his mouth. Rostam leapt up, drew his sword and attacked. Rakhsh bit Asdeev on the shoulder while Rostam beheaded the monster. Blood and poison streamed out of Asdeev, turning the earth into rock.

YONG

THE KIND DRAGON

WHO? Lucky bringer of wealth
WHAT? Bearded weather master
WHERE? Korea

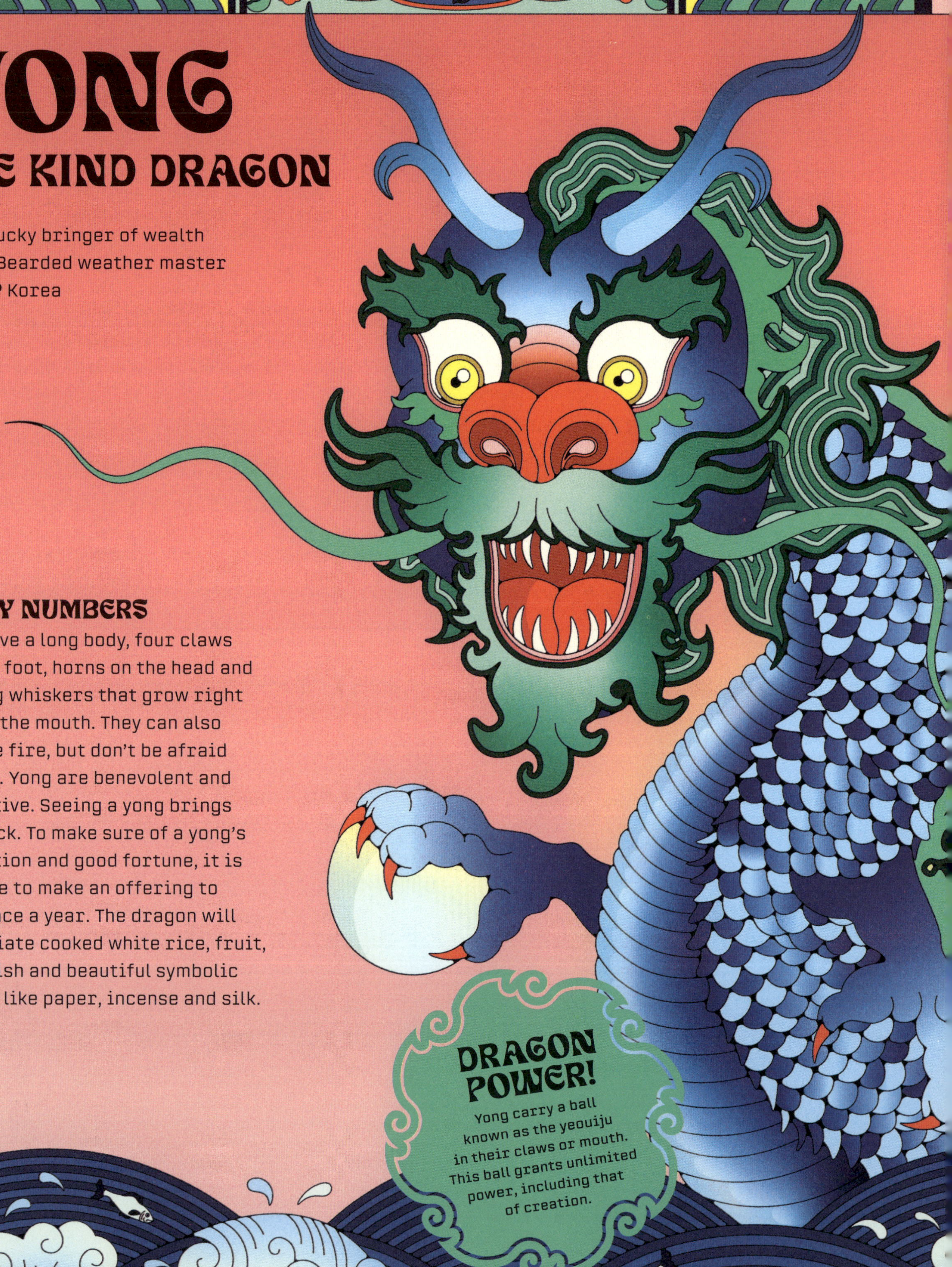

LUCKY NUMBERS

Yong have a long body, four claws on each foot, horns on the head and trailing whiskers that grow right around the mouth. They can also breathe fire, but don't be afraid of them. Yong are benevolent and protective. Seeing a yong brings good luck. To make sure of a yong's protection and good fortune, it is sensible to make an offering to them once a year. The dragon will appreciate cooked white rice, fruit, dried fish and beautiful symbolic objects like paper, incense and silk.

DRAGON POWER!

Yong carry a ball known as the yeouiju in their claws or mouth. This ball grants unlimited power, including that of creation.

BECOMING A DRAGON

Any creature can become a yong, though they usually start life as large, hornless python-like creatures known as imugi. These are lesser dragons. To become a true dragon, or yong, they must live one thousand years and catch a yeouiju that has fallen from heaven. Only then do they grow horns, a fourth claw on each paw and their long, silky beards. With the growth of the fourth claw, yong can hold the orb, becoming wise and powerful.

WEATHERING THE FUTURE

The powers of the yong include an ability to manipulate the natural world, particularly the weather. They bring rain and fertility to the land, ending famine and drought. At sea, they help fishermen get a good catch and guide them in harnessing the wind and waves. When they rise up out of the water and climb beyond the clouds, they leave behind a rainbow.

NAGA
ROYAL DRAGON

WHO? Protector of the Buddha
WHAT? Water king
WHERE? Southeast Asia

MULTI-COLOURED ROYALTY

Nagas can be considered royalty as the first king married a female naga, resulting in a powerful lineage. Nagas live underwater, beneath lakes and rivers and sometimes in caves. There are four types of naga and they often have crowns or ruffs on their head, rows of shiny white teeth and shimmering scales. Some nagas have multiple heads. The more heads they have, the more powerful they are. But it is always an odd number of heads: three, five, seven or nine, never an even number.

DRAGON POWER!

Nagas may look powerful – and they are – but they are also spiritual protectors who guard against evil and ill wishes. They often appear on temple stairs and roofs to provide a bridge between the earth and the heavens.

GREAT BALLS OF FIRE

The mighty Mekong River that runs through Thailand and Laos is the home of Phaya Naga, a naga king. He controls the river, managing its flow and bringing prosperity to those who rely on its waters for their crops. Every year, people gather to set off fireworks and watch fireballs that the dragon sends up above the water as an offering to honour the Buddha.

SHELTER FROM THE STORM

When the Buddha was meditating under the Bodhi Tree, there was a great storm. It rained for seven days and nights. He was at risk of being swept away and drowned. But help came in the form of the mighty king of the nagas, Mucalinda. He coiled his body into seven circles and lifted the meditating Buddha above the flood. He also spread his seven heads over the Buddha to protect him from the rain.

DRAGON MUSEUM

There are many dragons to see across the world: dragons in temples, on textiles, in books and manuscripts, as carvings to be carried and flags to be waved. Turn the page to find out how and where to find these dragons.

LINDWORM

SOURCE:

Carved church doorway

The first written description of a Lindworm is in the 13th-century German epic poem *Das Nibelungenlied* (*Song of the Nibelungs*). This is one source of the story of Sigurd and Fafnir. The story also appears in the Norse *Völsunga saga*. There are carvings of the dragon in medieval Norwegian churches.

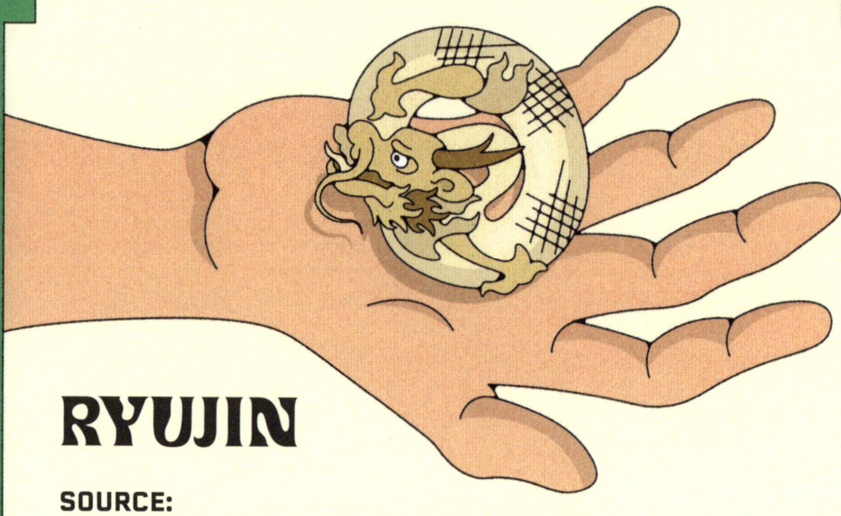

RYUJIN

SOURCE:

Carved kimono toggle

This dragon features in many stories over several centuries of Japanese history. His importance shows in the multiple forms of art that depict him: from tiny carved ivory kimono toggles (netsuke) to painted screens and ukiyo-e woodblock prints. He is worshipped in Shinto shrines across the country.

QUETZALCOATL

SOURCE:

Pictogram book *Codex Borbonicus*

Quetzalcoatl appears carved on the walls and steps of ancient Aztec and Maya temples. He is also represented in Aztec books, such as the *Codex Borbonicus*, which depicts him swallowing a man. Despite this, he represents the forces of good and light. The god shown with him, Tezcatlipoca, represents the opposing forces of evil and darkness.

HYDRA

SOURCE:

Pottery vase

The Hydra is first described in a poem by the ancient Greek author Hesiod in the 8th century BCE. But it was Euripides the playwright who first mentioned Hydra's ability to grow back a head for each one that Hercules severed. This battle is shown on several ancient vases.

LONG

SOURCE:

Ceramic-tiled wall

These dragons have been central to Chinese culture and history for thousands of years. The earliest sculpture of a long dates to the 4th century BCE. Their links with the emperors can be found in the dragons embroidered on imperial robes and the nine-dragon ceramic tiled wall in the Forbidden City, Beijing.

DRAC

SOURCE:
Oil painting

Drac is known through stories of Catalan folklore (Catalonia is a region in Spain). His nemesis, St Jordi, is the patron saint of Catalonia. The killing of Drac by St Jordi is the subject of several Catalan paintings from the late medieval period onwards. Effigies of this dragon are created and carried in festivals in the region.

AIDO-HWEDO

SOURCE:
Sculpture

This dragon was the assistant to the creator deity Mawu-Lisa and is a powerful spirit still worshipped in Benin, West Africa. The history of this dragon has been passed down orally through generations. There is a sculpture of Aido-Hwedo holding her tail in her mouth in Kpasse Sacred Forest, Ouidah, Benin.

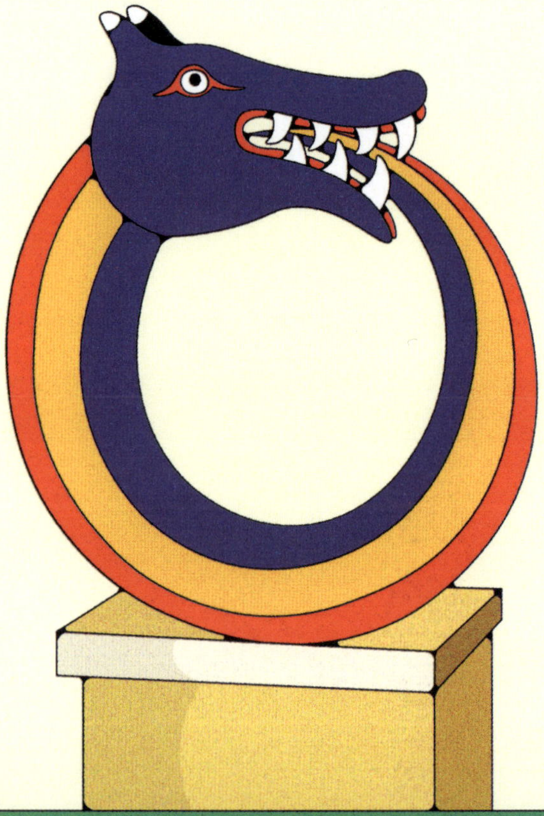

Y DDRAIG GOCH

SOURCE:
Hand-written book *Le Roman de Brut*

This red dragon and the battle at Dinas Emrys appear in *The Mabinogion* (a collection of Welsh stories). It also appears in earlier histories of Britain. One of these was the Anglo-Norman *Le Roman de Brut*. A 14th-century manuscript of this includes an illustration of the fighting dragons.

LEVIATHAN

SOURCE:

Hand-written book of beasts

Leviathan can be found in the Hebrew Bible and in the Christian Old Testament of the Bible. The Book of Job describes this fearsome dragon of the sea with his ability to breathe fire and his impenetrable scales. There are medieval miniatures and illustrations of this mighty creature in Hebrew bestiaries.

DRACO

SOURCE:

Hand-written book of beasts

The tales of draco date back to the ancient Romans. It was the Roman author Pliny the Elder who first wrote the recipe for the anti-dragon nettle rub! This was then rewritten in medieval bestiary manuscripts of the 13th century, where draco's hatred of elephants was also described and illustrated.

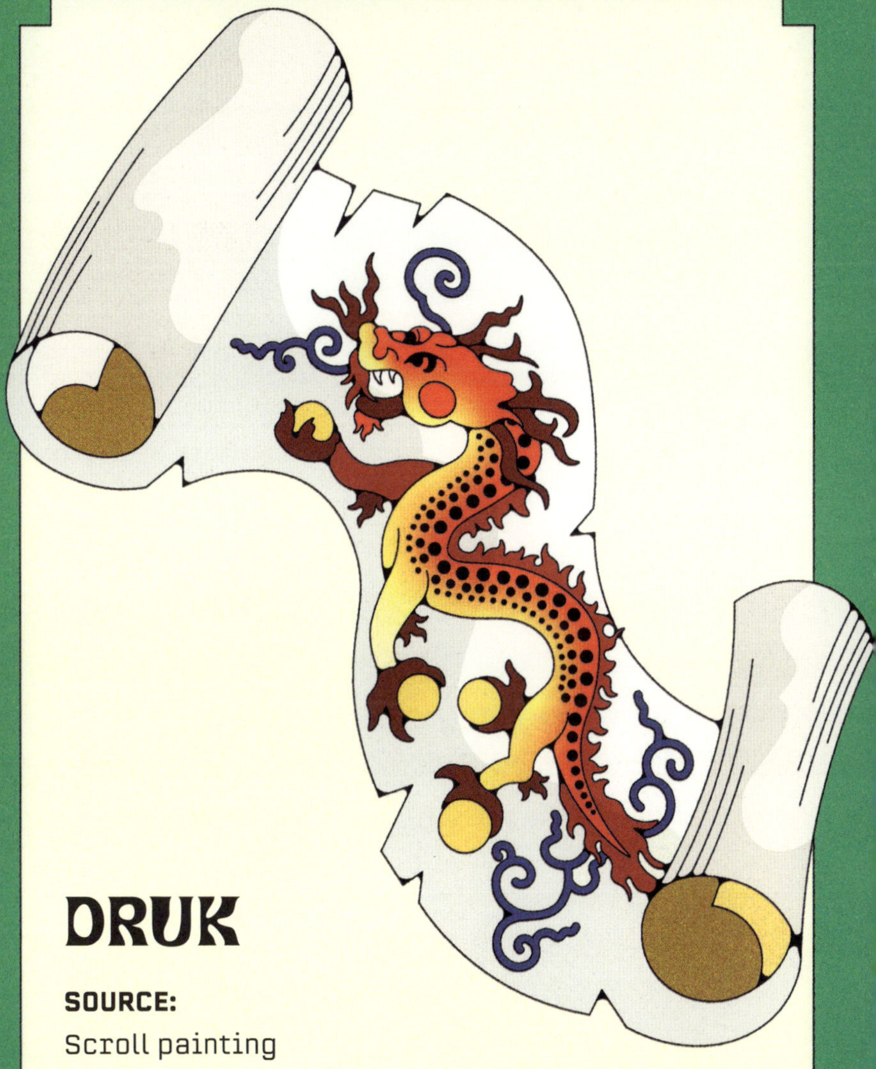

DRUK

SOURCE:

Scroll painting

Bhutan has been the land of the thunder dragon since the 12th century. Druk is so important to the history and Buddhist culture of Bhutan that images of him appear everywhere. He appears in scroll paintings, is painted on the walls of houses, carved into wooden pillars and above doors, and even appears on the national flag.

TANIWHA

SOURCE:

Bone carving pendant

These dragons of Aotearoa New Zealand are as old as the history of the Māori people. The dragons came to the islands with the first inhabitants. Individual taniwha are carved into the posts of meeting houses and onto pendants. They are revered as guardian spirits and protectors of places.

AZHDAHA

SOURCE:

Hand-written book

These central Asian dragons feature in many Persian stories. Especially in *Shahnameh* by Ferdowsi, an epic poem that tells of the history of Persia from the creation of the world to the Muslim conquest in the 7th century. Many of the manuscripts of the *Shahnameh* include miniature paintings of heroes battling dragons.

YONG

SOURCE:

Porcelain vase

Stories and images of these dragons have been shared in Korea for centuries. One of the earliest is a tomb painting from the ancient Goguryeo dynasty from the 5th century. They also appear in scroll paintings, on vases, textiles, ceramic tiles and murals, and carved into Buddhist halls and temples.

NAGA

SOURCE:

Temple stair sculpture

There are many nagas in South and Southeast Asia, where they are often associated with lakes and rivers. They are revered in both Hinduism and Buddhism, with descriptions in the written texts of both religions. Depictions of nagas with crests or crowns and shimmering scales appear sculpted on pathways and roofs of temples and religious buildings.

GLOSSARY

Ancient Very old or from very long ago.

Bestiaries Books that list and describe different creatures.

The Buddha A man called Siddhartha Gautama who achieved enlightenment and founded the teachings of Buddhism.

Celestial Relating to the heavens or the night sky.

Chaos A state of confusion and disorder where nothing makes sense.

Constellation A named group of stars in the sky that form a pattern or picture.

Creator A being of great power that can create things such as entire universes or worlds out of nothing.

Drought A long period of time when there is less rain than is normal, leading to a very dry landscape and water shortage.

Epic A very long narrative poem that recounts a hero's feats.

Evil To be morally bad and wicked.

Famine An extreme shortage of food that leads to a hunger crisis.

Fatal Causing death.

Fertility The ability to create new life.

Folklore A traditional story that is passed down through generations.

Fortune A person's luck as they navigate life.

Guardian A protector of something or someone.

Heaven A place in the sky, some believe it is where people go when they die or where gods live.

Hoard A large amount of something valuable, usually hidden away.

Imperial Belonging to the emperor that rules the country.

Indigenous Someone descended from or something belonging to the earliest known inhabitants of a country or area of land. For example, Māori people are indigenous to Aotearoa New Zealand and te reo is one of their indigenous languages.

Kimono A loose-fitting garment in Japanese culture that wraps around the wearer and ties at the waist with a sash.

Lair A shelter or resting place for a wild animal, usually well hidden.

Legend A very old or well-remembered story about a person or event.

Lineage A long line of family descended from one common ancestor.

Manuscript A hand-written book or document.

Medieval A specific period in history, from the 5th century to the 14th century.

Meditation A spiritual practice that requires mental and physical concentration.

Monk A male person who dedicates their life to a religion.

Myth A very old, traditional story that often explains how things were created and came into being.

Offering To give an object of value as a sign of respect or as a gift.

Pictogram Pictures that convey meaning to the reader – the Aztec people didn't have a writing system so they used pictograms instead.

Sacrifice To give something up, often something valuable, for a specific cause.

Saga A long narrative of heroic deeds.

Serpentine Resembling a serpent or a snake in appearance.

Servant A person who does someone else's bidding.

Shape-changer Something that can change its physical form into something else.

Shrine A place of significance where people go to worship or pay their respects.

Spirit A supernatural being that is not of our physical world.

Tribe A group of people that live together as a community and share the same beliefs and culture.

Typhoon A huge storm with strong and violent winds.

Underworld An underground world where some believe people will go when they die.

Worship To show respect, gratitude or awe towards something.

INDEX

A
air 16
Asdeev 33
Aztec 13, 40, 46

B
beard 10, 17, 34–35
bestiaries 27, 43, 46
the Buddha 36–37, 46

C
Catalonia 18–19, 42
claw 7, 8, 10, 17, 18, 28, 34–35
creator 12–13, 21, 28, 32, 42, 46

D
Dinas Emrys 22–23, 42
drought 16, 35, 46

F
Fafnir 9, 40
feathers 12
fire 7, 18, 24, 27, 32, 34, 37, 43

I
imugi 35

H
Han Dynasty 17
Hercules 15, 41
Himalayas 7, 28

K
kilbit 25
Korea 34, 45

L
lair 23, 30, 46
Lludd 23

M
Māori 31, 44, 46
Mawu-Lisa 21, 42
Merlin 22–23,
mountain 20–21, 28

O
ocean 7, 10–11, 16, 21, 24, 31

P
pearl 10, 16
poison 9, 14–15, 26–27, 33
protect 7, 9, 11, 13, 15, 18, 27, 29, 30–31, 34, 36–37, 44, 46

R
Rostam 33

S
sacrifice 13, 18, 46
sea 10–11, 16, 24, 30, 35, 43
serpent 7, 8, 10, 12, 14, 20, 46
scales 7, 9, 12, 17, 25, 36, 43, 45
Sigurd 9, 40
stink 18, 24
storm 11, 17, 28–29, 37, 46
St Jordi 18–19, 42

T
teeth 12, 18, 24, 30, 36
treasure 7, 8–9

U
underworld 13, 14, 46

V
Vortigern 22

W
water 10, 14, 16, 30–31, 35, 36–37, 46
wings 8, 18, 26, 32

ABOUT THE AUTHOR AND ILLUSTRATOR

Sally A. Nicholls

Sally A. Nicholls is a picture researcher and editor who works for *History Today*. For this book she conducted her research both in libraries and archives and during her own intrepid travels, bringing together a global cast of dragons from a range of cultures and locations.

Maria Francesca Melis

Maria Francesca Melis is an illustrator and designer who splits her time between her native Sardinia in Italy and New Zealand. She was a shortlisted artist in the 2025 AOI World Illustration Awards.

Thank you to all the consultants who so generously shared their expertise with us: Bella Myŏng-wŏl Dalton-Fenkl, Heinz Insu Fenkl, Zara Fleming, Alexandra Green, Nicole-Rachelle Moore, Joe Nickols, Tania Roxborogh and Antony Wynn.

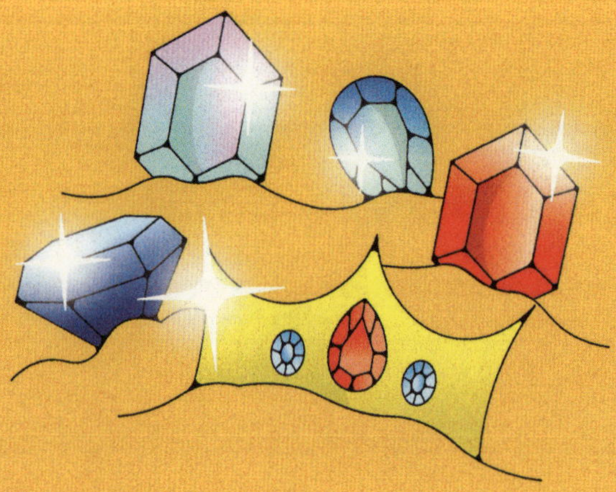